The New
Friend Fix

WITHDRAWN

Don't miss Catalina's other magical adventures!

Catalina Incognito
Off-Key

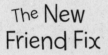

BY JENNIFER TORRES

CATALINA INCOGNITO

The New Friend Fix

ILLUSTRATED BY
GLADYS JOSE

ALADDIN
New York London Toronto Sydney New Delhi

This book is a work of fiction. Any references to historical events, real people, or real places are used fictitiously. Other names, characters, places, and events are products of the author's imagination, and any resemblance to actual events or places or persons, living or dead, is entirely coincidental.

ALADDIN

An imprint of Simon & Schuster Children's Publishing Division

1230 Avenue of the Americas, New York, New York 10020

First Aladdin paperback edition March 2022

Text copyright © 2022 by Jennifer Torres

Illustrations copyright © 2022 by Gladys Jose

Also available in an Aladdin hardcover edition.

All rights reserved, including the right of reproduction in whole or in part in any form.

ALADDIN and related logo are registered trademarks of Simon & Schuster, Inc.

For information about special discounts for bulk purchases, please contact Simon & Schuster Special Sales at 1-866-506-1949 or business@simonandschuster.com.

The Simon & Schuster Speakers Bureau can bring authors to your live event. For more information or to book an event contact the Simon & Schuster Speakers Bureau at 1-866-248-3049 or visit our website at www.simonspeakers.com.

Designed by Laura Lyn DiSiena

The illustrations for this book were rendered digitally.

The text of this book was set in Century Schoolbook.

Manufactured in the United States of America 0122 OFF

2 4 6 8 10 9 7 5 3 1

Library of Congress Control Number 2021937747

ISBN 9781534483071 (hc)

ISBN 9781534483064 (pbk)

ISBN 9781534483088 (ebook)

FOR MY GRANDFATHER, VALDEMAR ESPINOZA,

WHO KNOWS THE MAGIC OF A GOOD STORY

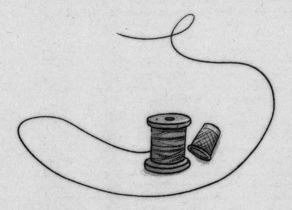

Contents

· CHAPTER 1 ·

First Day

1 have already slurped the last sugary drops of cereal milk off my spoon by the time my big sister, Coco, stumbles to the table.

She yawns and rubs her eyes, then asks, "You're already dressed, Cat?"

"Of course I am." It's the first day of school, after all. Last night I spent two hours organizing my backpack, filling the pouches and pockets with freshly sharpened pencils, never-used erasers, and notebooks with nothing but blank pages inside. Everything is perfectly put together.

Stuffing a backpack with new school supplies is one of my all-time favorite activities. Which means the day before school starts is one of my all-time favorite days of the year.

"But it's so early," Coco whines.

"It's never too early to be prepared," I answer.

Papi sets a bowl of cereal in front of Coco while I carry my empty bowl to the sink.

"Buenos días!" he greets her.

"Ugh," Coco moans.

Baby Carlos, our little brother, bangs his palms against his high-chair tray, and Papi drops a few chunks of strawberry onto it. Carlos picks one up and mashes it in his fist.

Even though his sticky hands can't reach me, I still take a big step backward. Just in case.

Mami walks into the kitchen dressed in purple scrubs, all set for her shift at the nursing home.

"Are you excited to start middle school?" she asks, ruffling Coco's sleep-tangled hair.

Coco shrugs.

No one asks if I'm excited to start third grade. Maybe they think it will be just like any other year. Unlike Coco, I'm not going to a new school. But there will still be a new classroom, a new teacher, and—according to my best friend, and biggest rival, Pablo Blanco—a new kid. He heard all about her because his mom is the room parent.

Just one more reason to get to school early. Then *I'll* get to meet the new girl before anyone else does. Even Pablo.

I check to make sure my double-knotted shoelaces haven't come undone, then swing my backpack over my shoulder.

"See you later!" I announce.

Carlos gurgles and waves his gooey hand. Mami and Papi walk over to hug me goodbye.

"Have a wonderful day, mija," Papi says.

"I can't wait to hear all about it," Mami adds, and kisses my forehead.

"Wait!" Coco's mouth is full of frosted wheat squares. "What's the hurry? Give me a few more minutes, and I'll walk with you. Like always."

My hand hovers over the doorknob. Coco and I used to walk to school together every day. But I never thought she actually *wanted* to.

"But we don't go to the same school anymore, remember?" I say, turning the knob.

"We can walk to the corner at least," Coco persists. "I'll even let you ride my skateboard."

Hmm. Coco has been teaching me to ride her skateboard all summer. But only in front of our house. She's never offered to let me ride it anywhere else before.

Even Mami and Papi are surprised.

"Did you hear that, Kitty-Cat?" Papi asks. "Coco says you can ride her skateboard!"

I am tempted to tell Coco yes.

I am tempted to tell Papi to quit calling me "Kitty-Cat."

But, *no*, I decide. There isn't time. I need to get to school. I only have one chance to be the first person to meet the new girl. Then I'll get to introduce her to everyone else. Maybe our teacher will even pick me to show her around school.

"Thanks anyway, Coco," I say. "Maybe tomorrow."

I am stepping out the door when Coco stops me *again*.

"You're wearing *that*?"

My shoulders drop. I hoped no one would notice.

"Didn't you say you were getting too old for all the kitten stuff?" Coco continues.

Slowly I turn around. Coco is pointing at the gray sweatshirt tied around my waist. Two kitten ears and a diamond-shaped patch of white fur are sewn to the hood.

"At least I don't sleep in it too," I say, pointing back at the old flannel shirt Coco *never* takes off.

Coco straightens the collar. "This shirt is *lucky*."

"Well, this sweatshirt," I answer, "is . . . *special*."

"That's right," Mami says. She wraps her arm around my shoulders and squeezes. "Tía Abuela sewed the ears on herself. And I'm sure Kitty-Cat likes wearing it because she misses Tía Abuela. Isn't that right?"

I nod. Tía Abuela is my great-aunt. Her name is Catalina Castañeda just like mine. She used to be a famous telenovela actress. Ever since she retired, Tía Abuela spends most of her time traveling the world. She doesn't come to our house on the hill in Valle Grande very often, so I *do* miss her.

But that's not the only reason why this sweatshirt is special.

On her last visit Tía Abuela gave me a musty old sewing kit in a red velvet pouch. Inside is a needle and a spool of silvery thread. They don't sew regular clothes, though. They create magical disguises. Like this sweatshirt. As soon as I zip it up and pull on the hood, I'll look exactly like an *actual* cat. Over the summer I even used my disfraz to solve a major mystery. So far I haven't shared the secret of the sewing kit with *anyone*.

Before she left on her latest adventure, Tía Abuela warned me that the magic would only be as strong as my stitches. Since I'm still learning, I haven't been able to sew a new disfraz yet. That's why I'm stuck with this one. Even if I *am* getting too old for all this kitten stuff.

I look down at my watch. "Better go," I say. "You know how I feel about being late."

Mami and Papi shudder. Even Coco stops arguing.

I smile to myself and scamper down the front porch steps and out to the sidewalk. Once I'm a few houses down, where I'm sure my family can't see me, I duck behind a mailbox.

I look left and right to make sure no one is watching. I put on the sweatshirt and zip it to my chin.

Then I lift the hood over my head. A chill runs up my spine.

I stand and glance down at my shadow on the pavement. It's not the shadow of a girl anymore. It's the shadow of a cat.

I am *incognito*.

CHAPTER 2

THE NEW GIRL

I prowl Valle Grande Elementary School, hoping to catch a glimpse of the new girl before anyone else does.

I dart from behind the drinking fountain to a playground bench. Peering out from underneath, I watch kids pose for pictures next to the school sign. Red and gold balloons bob on either side of it, and black letters on the front spell out "Welcome Back!"

The *B* is a little bit crooked, though. Someone

should have used a ruler! I wish I could ignore it, but I can't. In fact, I am so distracted that I don't notice Mr. Clark, the school custodian, walking toward me with a push broom until he's crouching right in front of my nose.

"You don't belong here," he says gently. "Someone might be allergic."

Uh-oh. I scramble backward, then dash for the school garden.

"Hey, wait!" Mr. Clark calls after me.

I dive between two tomato plants and hide behind a tangle of leaves. Luckily for me, someone drops a thermos full of macaroni and cheese on the ground, and Mr. Clark stops to help clean it.

I let my breath out slowly and shakily. That new

girl better get here soon. I need to change out of this disfraz before the bell rings—and before I get caught.

Finally I spot her: a girl about my age who I've never seen at school before. She has two long braids, round glasses, and a sprinkle of freckles across her nose.

But she isn't alone. She's walking—and talking!— with Jazmín Galindo, another third grader. How could Jazmín have met the new girl first? Even worse, *Pablo* is speeding toward them!

I'm about to leap from the garden box, when I remember I am still incognito. As quickly as I can, I yank off my hood and pat down my hair. When I'm certain no one is looking, I climb out.

By the time I catch up with Jazmín and the new girl, Pablo is already introducing himself. Or, at least he's trying to.

"Buenos días," Pablo says, holding out his hand. "I'm Pab—"

Instead of stopping, Jazmín walks even faster. "Come on." She takes the new girl by the wrist and pulls her toward the third-grade classroom, leaving Pablo and me behind.

Pablo folds his arms. He's wearing his usual crisp, white guayabera and gleaming white sneakers. "That was not very polite," he says, watching Jazmín and the new girl hurry away from us.

I shake my head. "It certainly was not."

Then Pablo sniffs. He wrinkles his nose. "You smell like a tomato."

I huff. "Don't be ridiculous." But when Pablo looks away, I shake out my hair just in case there are any more tomato leaves stuck in there.

We walk together the rest of the way to class.

Ms. Coleman, our new teacher, has placed a small clay flowerpot on each desk. Our names are painted on them, and instead of a plant inside, there are a pair of scissors, a glue stick, and a cactus-shaped bookmark that says *Keep growing!*

Very well-organized! I think.

I find the flowerpot with my name on the desk

behind Pablo's. *Alphabetical order!* I can already tell I'm going to like Ms. Coleman.

As I sit down, I sneak a glance at the new girl's desk in the next row over, right in front of Jazmín's. Her flowerpot says "Esmeralda."

I feel a tap on my shoulder and turn around.

"Have you met the new girl?" Aaron Chu whispers.

"Not exactly," I say. "Have you?"

He shakes his head. "No, but on the way to school this morning, I saw her leaving Jazmín's house."

Pablo spins around. "She was at *Jazmín's* house?"

The bell rings before Aaron can answer. Everyone stops talking. Pablo and I turn to face Ms. Coleman, who is smiling in front of the whiteboard.

"Good morning, third graders," she says. "I hope you're as excited as I am to start this amazing year. I look forward to getting to know each and every one of you. But I want to take a moment to welcome one student in particular. Everyone, meet Esmeralda. She's new to our school this year."

All of us look at the new girl. Her cheeks turn pink, and she twists one of her braids around her finger.

"Esmeralda, we're so glad you're here," Ms. Coleman says. "Would you like to stand and tell us all a little about yourself?"

Esmeralda doesn't answer. She stares down at her lap and keeps twisting her braid.

Some kids start to whisper. Pablo looks over his shoulder at me. *Qué pasa?* he mouths.

I shake my head. I have no idea what's going on. Maybe she's just really nervous?

"Esmeralda?" Ms. Coleman asks again, gently.

Jazmín's hand shoots up. "Ms. Coleman?"

"Yes, Jazmín?"

Jazmín looks around at all of us staring back at her and Esmeralda.

"Esmeralda is my cousin. We call her 'Esme.' She just moved here with her parents—they're staying at my house—and she's pretty shy, that's all."

Ms. Coleman nods. "Thank you, Jazmín. The first day at a brand-new school *can* be a little scary. But I know you'll all help Esme feel right at home."

I think I see Esme's lips twitch up into what might be a tiny smile. But then Jazmín turns and glares straight at Pablo and me.

"That means you two," she growls. "Don't pick on my cousin."

Pablo and I gasp.

CHAPTER 3

Mean Jazmín

*M*s. Coleman's eyes widen.

She looks at Pablo, then at me. "I'm sure I can count on both of you to be extra kind to Esme, right?"

"Yes," we mumble. My cheeks burn. I can't believe Jazmín said that in front of everyone! In front of Ms. Coleman! Now Ms. Coleman thinks Pablo and I are *mean*. I am so upset, I could yowl. Exactly like a cat whose tail has been trampled on.

Pablo is angry too. I can tell because his shoulders

are so tense that they're almost touching his ears. I am now determined to make Esme our new best friend. It's the only way to prove Jazmín wrong and show Ms. Coleman she really *can* count on us.

So, later that morning, when I notice that Esme's pencil is a little dull, I lean over and whisper, "It looks like you need a sharper point. You can use one of mine." I try to give her one of my perfectly sharpened pencils, but Jazmín sticks out her hand and blocks me.

"I *said*, leave my cousin alone!" she hisses. "There's nothing wrong with her pencil!"

Then, when we're lining up for recess, Pablo notices that one of the ribbons at the end of Esme's braid has come loose.

"I can fix it for you," he offers. "I happen to be an expert at knots."

It's true. I learned my shoelace technique from Pablo. Not that I'd ever admit it.

But Esme doesn't answer. She bites her lip and looks down.

Jazmín scowls.

"Don't listen to them," she tells Esme, leading her away. "They think they're *so* perfect, but they're not."

Pablo crosses his arms. "That was uncalled for."

"You were only trying to help," I agree.

By lunchtime we are out of ideas. Esme won't talk to us, let alone get to know us.

"It's all because of Jazmín," I grumble, picking the burnt spots off my bean burrito. Mami always thinks I won't notice if the burnt parts are on the inside of the tortilla. But I do.

"More like *Mean* Jazmín," he says. "What did we ever do to her?" He tears another bite off his ham-and-cheese sandwich.

We chew quietly, watching the lunch table where Esme is sitting with Jazmín and her friends. Esme takes a sip from her juice box, then pokes at her cucumber-and-watermelon salad.

"Maybe it's not just us," I observe.

Pablo stops chewing. He swallows. He dabs the corner of his mouth with a napkin. "What do you mean?"

I nod toward Esme. "She isn't talking to *anyone*. Maybe Jazmín was telling the truth, and she's shy. Or maybe . . . she doesn't like it here."

Pablo tilts his head. His eyes glimmer with a new idea.

"Or maybe," he says, "it's something *else. . . .*" His voice trails off mysteriously.

"Something else?"

Pablo uses his napkin to sweep sandwich crumbs off the table and into his empty lunch bag. Once his trash is folded into a neat pile, he drops his head and leans in closer.

"Maybe," he says, his voice low, "Jazmín won't let Esme make any friends. Maybe Esme is trapped. It's just like what happened in this telenovela my mom and I are watching, *Secrets of the Castle.*"

I groan. Pablo is a telenovela aficionado, which means he's a huge fan of these dramatic, Spanish-language television shows. The ones Tía Abuela used to act in. He can get a little carried away.

"No, listen," Pablo insists. "It's about a young

duchess who gets sent far from home to live with her aunt to learn how to rule. Except the aunt keeps the duchess locked in the castle and won't let her speak to anyone because the aunt is secretly scheming to take over and become the duchess herself." By the time Pablo finishes, he is nearly out of breath.

I hand him his water bottle. "I'm pretty sure Esme isn't a duchess, Pablo," I say.

Pablo sighs. "I *know* she is not a duchess. But that doesn't mean Jazmín isn't trying to keep her from making friends."

That *might* explain why Jazmín keeps getting in the way every time we try to do something nice for Esme. "But why wouldn't Jazmín want her cousin to have friends?"

Pablo drums his fingers on the table. "We won't know for sure until we investigate."

Suddenly Jazmín stands. For a second I worry

she's overheard us talking about her. My heart races. But then she pulls a stack of envelopes from her backpack. "My mom is throwing a get-to-know-you tardeada for Esme this weekend," she announces.

"A what?" I whisper to Pablo. I'm pretty good at Spanish, but Pablo is better. Maybe from watching all those telenovelas.

"A tar-deh-AH-dah," he repeats slowly. "An afternoon party."

"We hope you can come," Jazmín continues. She starts to pass out invitations, handing one to every third grader in the cafeteria.

But when she gets to the table Pablo and I are sitting at, she walks right by, dropping our invitations back into her bag.

· CHAPTER 4 ·

ЅOMETHING ᛗAGICAL

ᛗaybe she didn't see us," I suggest. But even I know that's impossible.

"Or maybe," Pablo replies, "she knows we're onto her scheme."

Either way, we have to snag those invitations. We agree that after school each of us will spend thirty minutes thinking up a plan. It will have to wait until after I've had a snack, reorganized my backpack, done my homework, and laid out my clothes for tomorrow, though. I have a schedule to keep, after all.

But when I get home, there's an *unscheduled* delay. "Kitty-Cat, is that you?" Papi calls out as I'm stepping inside. "You're just in time!"

I follow Papi's voice to the living room. His laptop is open on the coffee table, and Carlos is clapping into the camera. *Just in time for this?* One of Carlos's baby videos? Then I hear a cackle that can only belong to one person.

"Tía Abuela!" I shout. I drop my backpack in the middle of the floor—which Coco does all the time, but not me—and race to the computer.

"Catalina, ahí estás!" Tía Abuela smiles back at me on Papi's computer screen.

"Here I am!" I echo. As usual, Tía Abuela is wearing her cat-eye sunglasses with sparkling crystals on the frames. There seems to be a snowstorm behind

her. I lean in closer to the screen. "But where are *you*? Aren't you supposed to be in the Galápagos?"

Tía Abuela laughs. "Por favor! I left Isla Isabela weeks ago. I'm in Chile. Near Cerro Castillo."

The video blurs and wobbles. When Tía Abuela comes back into focus, I notice her earrings. "Are those new?" I ask. "They look like orange blossoms."

Tía Abuela pulls back the hood of her fuzzy parka to give me a better look. "You don't miss a thing, do you, Kitty-Cat?" she asks, and then chuckles.

Nope. I have excellent attention to detail. "They remind me of the orange tree in our backyard," I say.

"Sí, me too," Tía Abuela replies. "That's why I bought them. I was beginning to miss Valle Grande and wanted something that reminded me of home. That's also why I called. Tell me everything! How was the first day of school?"

I want to tell her all about Esme and Mean

Jazmín. Tía Abuela could help me untangle this problem the way she helped me learn to thread a needle and sew my first messy stitches.

I glance over at Papi. He's helping Carlos build a tower with rainbow-colored blocks. You're supposed to put the biggest ones on the bottom of the stack, but their tower is all jumbled and about to topple over.

Even though he looks busy, there's still a chance Papi might be listening, so I don't tell Tía *everything*.

"Well, there's a new girl in our class," I begin. "Her name is Esme. Pablo and I are trying to make friends with her, but it isn't working. I don't think she even *wants* to be our friend."

Tía Abuela presses her lips together and hums. "Pues," she says after a while. "Don't be so quick to think you know how Esme feels. It's like that old saying, 'Caras vemos, corazones no sabemos.'"

She repeats the saying in English to make sure

I understand: "Faces we can see, but hearts we do not know."

It *almost* sounds as if Tía Abuela agrees with Pablo. Like she thinks something else is going on. Something secret.

"Why don't you tell my comadre Josefina about your problem?" Tía Abuela suggests. "You'll see her this afternoon at the Stitch and Share meeting, no?"

I try to make my sigh as quiet as possible, but even thousands of miles away, Tía Abuela can hear it. She pulls her glasses to the bottom of her nose and raises one eyebrow. "You didn't think I'd forget, did you?"

I guess I'm not the only one with excellent attention to detail. After she gave me the sewing pouch and my first lessons, Tía Abuela made me promise to go to the weekly Stitch and Share sessions that her best friend, Josefina, hosts at the Valle Grande

Central Library. That way, I'd get more practice.

"But the only things Josefina ever lets me sew are pillowcases!" I argue. "I'm ready to move on to something new." I move closer to the computer screen and whisper, "Something *magical*."

Tía Abuela pushes her glasses back up to the bridge of her nose. She waves off my complaint with a flutter of her long, pink fingernails.

"Just go to the meeting, Kitty-Cat," she says finally. "You might learn something—and not just about sewing. You'd better hurry or you're going to be late. And we all know how you feel about being late."

I gulp and check my watch. She's right.

· CHAPTER 5 ·

STITCH AND SHARE

Josefina the Librarian looks up from the dog toy she's stitching when I walk into the Valle Grande Central Library community room. I am huffing and puffing after sprinting all the way down the hill from my house to get here.

It is exactly two minutes before the Stitch and Share meeting is scheduled to start. In other words, I am right on time.

"Prompt as usual, Catalina," Josefina says. She

sets down her sewing project and stands to greet me.

"What do you think about working on a *pillow-case* today?" Her eyes sparkle when she says "pillow-case." As if it's the most exciting project ever. As if I haven't already sewn four of them.

The metal folding chairs in the community room are arranged in a circle. At the center is a big plastic bin filled with scraps of fabric donated by library visitors. Josefina opens the bin and begins rummaging through the cloth. She digs through flower prints, polka dots, stripes.

I take a step toward her. "I do love pillowcases," I say, peering into the bin. "But now I think I'm ready for something different. Something a little more . . . challenging."

And interesting, I want to add. But I don't. What I'd really like to sew is a new disfraz. If I could disguise myself as a magician or a party princess, I might be able to sneak into Esme's tardeada even without an invitation.

But I know Josefina the Librarian would never let me work on something *that* interesting.

"Here it is!" Josefina announces as if she hasn't heard me at all. "As soon as I saw it, I knew it would be perfect for you. Or should I say 'purrrfect'?'"

Josefina holds up a piece of fabric. It's pale blue and covered with kittens.

Of course.

Kittens playing with yarn balls. Kittens curled on blankets. Kittens with flowers behind their furry ears.

I want to tell her I'm getting too old for all this kitten stuff. But, the truth is, the fabric *is* kind of cute.

"It will make the *purrrfect* pillowcase," I admit. I take the fabric and choose a seat.

Josefina claps. "I knew you'd love it. The pattern reminds me of a calico kitten I used to foster. We called her 'Guapa' because she was so pretty. She used to love playing with yarn and ribbons."

It sounds like Josefina misses Guapa. I unfold the fabric and smooth it over my lap. "I could give you the pillowcase when I'm finished," I offer. "To remind you of Guapa."

Then I lower my voice and mutter, "I can *always* make another one."

Josefina pats my shoulder. "That would be delightful, Catalina. Gracias."

More people arrive at the Stitch and Share session. Josefina calls us sewists. I like the word because it sounds kind of like "artist." Everyone brings their latest project and shares what they're working on. If anyone runs into trouble, there are plenty of people to give advice. I get *lots* of advice.

Mrs. Glass, who always works on quilts, sits down next to me with her big wooden hoop. This time there is a patchwork of green and yellow squares stretched inside it.

"Who is it for?" I ask.

Mrs. Glass smiles as she takes the rest of her supplies out of her sewing bag. "It's for my nephew's family," she answers. "They're expecting a new baby."

Anthony Becerra sits down a few chairs over. Of all the sewists, he's the "closest" to my age—and he's in high school. Anthony is making dog and cat toys for the animal shelter as part of a community service project. Josefina and some of the other sewists have volunteered to help.

As everyone settles in, I open up my sewing kit—not the magic one, just an old cookie tin with needles and thread and other supplies inside. Tía Abuela gave it to me for practice. I choose a spool of thread that matches the blue kitten fabric, snip some off, and thread my needle.

When I first started sewing, it took me five or six tries to get the thread to slip through that teensy eye. Sometimes more. Now I do it on my first attempt.

Josefina notices. "Soon you'll be sewing quilts, just like Mrs. Glass," she says.

I'd settle for chew toys.

Josefina must be able to read my thoughts. Or maybe she can just read my face, because the next thing she says is, "I know you want to move faster, but your Tía Abuela told me it was very important that you learn to make your stitches nice and strong. And practice is the best way to make progress."

Ms. Yoo chuckles to herself.

"I was remembering the night I rushed through

sewing the buttons on a new dress so that I could make it to a party on time," she says. "Half of them fell off. I had to hold the dress together with staples!"

I feel my cheeks turn red, thinking about how embarrassing that must've been. I'd be in big trouble if a magical disfraz ever fell apart while I was wearing it.

"You think that's bad?" Mr. Hart pauses in the middle of a stitch. "You should hear about the time I decided to shorten my uniform pants. I didn't double-check the measurements, and one leg turned out longer than the other! I had to deliver the mail like that all day!"

I would have triple-checked the measurements. Still, I squint down at my stitches. Maybe a little more practice isn't such a bad idea. And while I sew, I can think up a way to make Esme see what a great friend I am.

CHAPTER 6

INCOGNITO

*T*he next afternoon Pablo and I creep behind a tree. We stare at Jazmín's backpack as she and Esme start walking home from school.

"Do you think our invitations are still in there?" he asks.

I nod. "I saw them when Jazmín took out her pencil case this morning."

Pablo unzips the front pocket of his backpack. He takes out two mango-flavored lollipops. He lowers his voice. "Here's what we're going to do. You run up and offer these to Jazmín and Esme. They probably won't take them. Jazmín might even yell at you to go away. While she's distracted, I'll sneak up behind her, open her backpack, and grab the invitations. It'll be just like a scene from *Diary of a Thief*!"

It's not that I don't like Pablo's plan. It's just that I have a better one. I came up with it during Stitch and Share. Only, I can't tell him about it because it involves my sweatshirt. *That* sweatshirt.

"Sorry, Pablo, but there's . . . something I need to do first," I reply. "Don't worry, though. We'll get those invitations."

"Don't *worry*?" he says. "The tardeada is this weekend. We don't have much time."

What can I say to convince him?

"I've already put the tardeada on my schedule," I say. "And if it's on my schedule—"

"You'll be there." Pablo finishes my sentence for me. "I hope you're right." He tucks the lollipops into his pocket and starts walking home.

Not until Pablo has turned the corner do I dare

to dig the kitten sweatshirt out of my backpack. I slip my arms inside, zip it up, and then put on the hood. Once again, I am incognito.

Disguised, I make my way to Jazmín's house.

When I get there, I find her and Esme outside, doing their homework on the front porch.

I duck behind a hedge in the Galindos' front yard and listen.

"What if no one comes?" Esme asks.

They're talking about the party! I poke my head out to hear better.

"Of course they'll come," Jazmín said. "I told you. I only invited the nice people."

Only invited the nice *people?*

I leap out from behind the hedge. "Hey! What's that supposed to mean?"

Except I'm still disguised as a cat, so it comes out like a snarl and a hiss.

Whoops.

Esme and Jazmín look up at the same time. I should probably run away while I still can. But I still need those invitations.

Esme points. "A cat!"

Jazmín frowns. "Shoo, go away. Mom doesn't like

cats in her plants." Typical. I'm starting to think Pablo is right. Jazmín *is* mean.

Esme stops writing and slowly walks down the front steps.

"Wait!" she says. "This cat looks familiar."

I do?

"She *does?*" Jazmín says.

Esme kneels on the grass, still giving me a lot of space. "Mm-hmm. She looks a lot like my neighbor's cat, León. León was a bit scruffy too."

"A bit *scruffy?*" I yowl. Even as a cat, I'm sure I am perfectly put together. I whisk some hair off my face.

"Look, she's cleaning herself!" Esme squeals, inching forward. "Isn't she so cute?"

Jazmín's frown softens. "She reminds you of your neighbor's cat? At your old house?" she asks. "Maybe we can get her to come closer."

Jazmín goes into the house and comes back with a can of tuna.

"Here, kitty," Jazmín says, waving the can at me.

I don't really like tuna. But this is my best chance to get close enough to Jazmín's backpack to snatch the invitations. I trot along the stone walkway, past Esme, up the steps, and onto the porch.

From here I can see what Esme has been working on. It's our spelling list. But instead of writing the words out five times each like Ms. Coleman told us to, Esme has been drawing a picture. It's a house with a red tile roof and a garden bursting with pink and orange roses.

Jazmín waves the can again. "Come on, kitty-cat, just a little closer."

I take another step. Then Jazmín says quietly, "As soon as I give her the tuna, you grab her and take her inside. Maybe my mom will let you keep her. To remind you of home."

Oh no! I whip my head around just as Esme is lunging for me, arms outstretched.

I leap out of the way. Esme screams as I scramble over the drawing, scattering her crayons.

Before I can catch my balance, Jazmín tries to grab me. I manage to duck under her arms, but not without knocking over her backpack. Everything spills out—pencils, pens, library books, and the two party invitations that were supposed to have gone to Pablo and me.

I dash down the steps right as Señora Galindo steps to the door. "What's going on out here?"

Then, as I race back out to the sidewalk, I hear her add, "Jazmín, I thought you said you handed out *all* the invitations."

CHAPTER 7

MESSY BUSINESS

That evening Papi takes his brown-bag dinner from the refrigerator, kisses Coco, Carlos, and me on our foreheads, and then leaves for the community college where he teaches a math class three nights a week.

"Adiós!" he says, and waves. "I'll see you all in the morning."

Coco and I set the table while Mami stirs a pot of fideo noodles on the stove. Carlos sits on the kitchen floor, jangling Mami's car keys.

"What's wrong with you?" Coco asks. "You've been in a bad mood ever since I got home."

I turn my head so Coco can't see my face. "Nothing."

Nothing except that I didn't get those invitations. And now they might not even be in Jazmín's backpack anymore.

But I don't feel like explaining everything to Coco, so I try to change the subject. "Shouldn't you be out skateboarding with your friends?"

Coco pulls her baseball cap so low on her forehead that I can't see her eyes anymore.

"Not in the mood," she says. "First I forgot my locker combination. Then I brought the wrong books to science class. And *then* I got lost on the way to history. *Again.* I wish I were back at Valle Grande Elementary, where I knew how everything worked."

It's strange to hear Coco sound nervous. She usually loves a new adventure. It takes me a long time to decide what to say.

"Well, it was only the second day," I tell her. "I bet it'll be exactly like learning a new skateboarding trick. At first you'll mess up a lot. But pretty soon it'll be like you were doing it forever."

Coco nudges me in the ribs. "I just hope I don't mess up as much as you do when you're learning a trick."

She is already starting to feel better. I can tell.

Coco lifts Carlos into his high chair, and I clear some space in the middle of the table for Mami to set down the soup pot. As soon as she does, her phone rings.

"You girls start feeding your brother," she says. "I'll be right back."

Both of us look at the soup spoon, but neither of

us reaches for it. Feeding Carlos is messy business. Especially when it comes to noodles.

"I think it's *your* turn," Coco says, spooning some fideo into his bowl before passing it to me.

"But he likes it better when *you* feed him," I insist, passing the bowl back.

Carlos screeches. In the hallway Mami covers the phone with her hand and shoots us a warning look.

"Niñas! Por favor!"

"We'll take turns," Coco offers. "You go first."

"Fine." I scoop some fideo into Carlos's mouth and try to move my hand away before half-chewed pieces of noodle and tomato land on it.

Mami holds the phone to her ear again. "I'm sorry, Rosa. What were you saying about a stray cat?"

Rosa? That's Jazmín's mom. I feed Carlos another bite of fideo and strain to listen.

"You know, we have been having some trouble with a stray cat too," Mami is saying. She pauses. "Sí! Gray with a diamond-shaped patch of white fur on her forehead. I wonder if it's the same cat!"

I drop Carlos's spoon, and it clatters onto his high-chair tray. I pick it up, wipe it off, and hand it to Coco. "Your turn."

Then I nod toward Mami and hold a finger up to my lips. Coco nods back. She'll keep quiet.

I tiptoe into the living room and toward the hallway to hear better.

"What a lovely way to make some friends," Mami says. "Oh, I see. . . . Ah. . . . Mm-hmm."

It is impossible to know what's going on when I can't hear Señora Galindo.

"Of course," Mami says. "You too. Goodbye!"

She clicks off the phone, and I bolt back to my chair.

Mami gets to the table moments later, and I

pretend I haven't been eavesdropping. "Who was that?" I ask.

Coco snorts.

Mami ignores her. "That was Señora Galindo. She's hosting a tardeada on Saturday so Jazmín's cousin Esme can get to know her classmates."

I scoot to the edge of my chair. I wait for Mami to say I'm invited.

But she doesn't.

She serves herself some fideo. She chews and swallows.

"Oh!" she says.

"Yes?" I answer, sitting up straighter. Here it comes. I bet she'll tell me now.

"I just had an idea," Mami continues. "What if I make Esme's parents a batch of my famous salsa verde?"

I slouch. Wrong again.

"I don't know," Coco teases. "We want to welcome them, not scare them away."

"Coco!" Mami presses her hand over her heart, pretending she's offended.

I actually *am* offended. "Why should we bring them anything if I wasn't even invited to the party?"

Mami winks. "Didn't you hear?" she asks. "Because I thought for sure I noticed someone listening near the hallway. Well. It turns out your invitation got misplaced by mistake. Jazmín will bring it to school tomorrow."

Looks like I managed to snag those invitations after all!

· CHAPTER 8 ·

Too Much

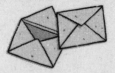

I can't wait to tell Pablo the good news. But when I spot him standing outside our classroom the next morning, I can see he already knows.

"Como el gato que se comió la manteca," I say as I walk up to him.

Pablo scrunches his nose. "Like the cat that ate the butter?" he asks. "What is that supposed to mean?" Then he sucks in a nervous breath and looks down at his shirt. "I didn't spill any butter on myself, did I?"

I laugh. "No, it's a saying Tía Abuela taught me. It means 'You look like you're very pleased with yourself.'"

Pablo grins. "As a matter of fact, I am." He opens his backpack and takes out his binder. Pablo has special dividers with tabs *and* pockets. I tried to convince Mami and Papi to buy me a set, but they said the last thing I need is more organizational supplies. If they could see how orderly Pablo's notebook is, I'm sure they'd change her minds.

Pablo flips to a tab near the back. He reaches into the pocket, pulls out an envelope, and hands it to me. "Open it."

"Let me guess," I say. "Is it an invitation to Esme's get-to-know-you tardeada?"

Pablo snatches the envelope back. "How'd you

know? Jazmín only gave it to me this morning."

I explain how Señora Galindo called Mami last night and how I'm getting an invitation too. "She says our invitations got misplaced by mistake."

We both know it was *not* a mistake.

"At least we get to go," he says. "Now all I need to do is find Esme the perfect welcome-to-the-neighborhood gift. Then she'll know Jazmín was wrong about me." He flips to another section of his notebook. "I've narrowed it down to five ideas."

I try to peek at Pablo's list, but he slams the notebook shut.

"Don't worry, I already have my *own* list," I fib. "And Esme's going to love *my* gift best."

I turn and march into the classroom.

Pablo follows close behind. "How can you be so sure you know what she likes? You've barely talked to her."

"Well, neither have you," I say as I take my seat.

Luckily, Ms. Coleman gives us a chance to fix that. Later that morning, when it's time for social studies, she divides the class into small groups. "Esme, why don't you join Catalina and Pablo?" she says.

We slide our desks over to make room, but Esme doesn't move. She looks down at the floor and twists one of her braids.

Jazmín raises her hand. "Ms. Coleman," she says before she's even called on. "Shouldn't Esme be in my group? Since she's my cousin?"

Pablo looks at me, eyes wide. "See? *Just* like *Secrets of the Castle*," he murmurs.

Ms. Coleman stands beside Jazmín's desk. "It's very thoughtful of you to look out for your cousin. But it will be good for Esme to make other friends too. And Catalina and Pablo will take good care of her." She turns to us. "Won't you?"

We nod eagerly. Finally Esme moves her desk toward ours.

Once everyone is in a group, Ms. Coleman gives the instructions. "First I want you to list the communities you belong to," she says. "As many as you can think of. Then, in your groups, talk about which communities you and your partners have in common."

I can't tell if Esme is listening. She's doodling at the edges of her notebook paper. It's the same house I saw in the drawing on the Galindos' porch, with pink and orange roses in the front. This time there's a gray cat next to it.

"All right, everyone," Ms. Coleman says. "Go ahead and get started, and let me know if you need any help."

Normally Pablo and I follow directions as carefully as we can. But this might be our only chance to get to know Esme before the tardeada, so we take it.

"I see you like to draw," Pablo says. "What kind of pencils are your favorite? Colored pencils? Mechanical pencils? Grease pencils?"

Esme hesitates. "I don't know," she mumbles without taking her eyes off her paper. "Just . . . regular pencils, I guess?"

Pablo scribbles something in his notebook.

"What about erasers?" I ask. Erasers are very important. They help you fix mistakes.

"Um . . . aren't they all sort of . . . the same?"

Esme says. Her voice is so quiet, I can hardly hear her.

Pablo smacks his hands against the desk. "All the same? But there's pink erasers and gum erasers and erasers you can roll up like clay—"

I interrupt him. Pablo can talk about erasers for hours. "What is that, anyway?" I ask, tapping the corner of Esme's paper. "Why do you keep drawing that house?"

Esme looks up. Her cheeks are

bright pink, and her eyes are shiny with tears.

"I don't know," she says. "I just like drawing it!"
Then she gets up and runs toward the door.

The whole class goes silent. Everyone stares at
Pablo and me. Jazmín jumps up from her seat and
glares at us.

"I knew this was going to happen!" she shouts.
"You're just too mean and too . . . *much*!"

· CHAPTER 9 ·

WHAT REALLY HAPPENED

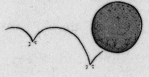

Ms. Coleman asks Pablo and me to stay in from recess. She calls us to her desk and folds her hands on top of it. I hold my breath.

"I know you didn't mean to hurt Esme's feelings," she tells us.

I let my air out, so relieved that my knees wobble. "We really didn't," I say.

"We were just trying to get to know her," Pablo

adds. "I don't know why she got so upset. I think it's Jazmín. She's—"

Ms. Coleman holds up a hand to stop us.

"I believe you. Just remember that Esme is new," Ms. Coleman says. "She's had to leave her home and her friends. And I think she might be a little sensitive. Give her some time to come out of her shell."

I'm glad Ms. Coleman believes us. Unfortunately, no one on the playground does.

"What did you say to Esme?" Aaron asks. "I know you two can be picky, but I thought you'd leave the new kid alone."

"We were *not* being picky," I protest. "We were only trying to plan the perfect present!" But Aaron isn't really listening.

Pablo and I walk over to the four-square courts. I love four square because there are rules that tell you what's allowed and what's not. But when we line up at the court, Gracie Davis grabs the ball and holds it under her arm. "Are you here to tell us we're doing it wrong? Just like you told Esme?"

"That is *not* what happened!" I say.

"According to Jazmín, it is," Bruno Zamora replies. "She said that you two were picking on Esme and her drawing and you made her cry."

This is so unfair. "Let's go, Pablo," I say. "We need to find Jazmín."

"You're right," he says. "This is all *her* fault. We need to figure out what she's up to before it gets worse. We have to warn Esme."

I'm pretty sure Pablo is wrong about Jazmín. After what I saw yesterday, I think she might be trying to protect Esme. We just need to explain that she doesn't have to protect her from *us*.

We find them on the climbing dome. I haven't played on it since first grade, when I hung upside down and my shirt slipped, and everyone saw my belly button.

Jazmín and Esme are sitting at the very top. I cup my hands around my mouth and call up to them.

"Can we talk to you?"

Jazmín turns to Esme. "Don't worry, I'll handle this." She scowls down at us. "What do you two want? Haven't you caused enough trouble?"

"Please?" I say. "We just want to explain what *really* happened in class earlier."

Jazmín jumps down from the climbing dome and lands in front of us.

"You don't have to explain anything," she says. "I already know what happened. You were picking on Esme's work the way you always do. It's just like in second grade, when you told me my dinosaur diorama was all wrong. I worked really hard on that!"

The dinosaur diorama? That was a whole year ago. And Pablo and I were only trying to help. I thought everyone wanted their project to be perfect.

"You had a stegosaurus and a tyrannosaurus together in your shoebox!" Pablo cries. "They lived in completely different periods. We thought you would want to know so you could fix it."

I would have wanted to know.

Jazmín turns her head away from us. "Well, it made me feel really bad. And I don't want you to make Esme feel bad too. I only gave you an invitation because Mom said I had to. But you are *not* welcome."

· CHAPTER 10 ·

A New Plan

I am so angry with Jazmín. For calling us mean. For refusing to listen when we tried to explain ourselves.

I'm even a little mad at Esme, too. I know she's new, but she could have said something. She knows Pablo and I weren't picking on her.

Doesn't she?

I try to imagine what Tía Abuela would do. She

wouldn't give up, that's for sure. She would think of a new plan.

It's amazing how many problems you can solve with a needle and thread, Tía Abuela once told me. And I start to wonder if sewing can fix this situation.

I've got it, I decide as I march home from school. *I'll use the magic sewing kit to create a* hornet *disfraz to wear to Esme's party*. No one will be able to enjoy the tardeada with me buzzing around. The party will be completely ruined.

But by the next morning, I don't really feel like scheming anymore. Jazmín should have given Pablo and me a chance to tell our side of the story. But maybe *we* should have stopped to think about how all our attention to detail makes others feel. Especially someone who doesn't know us very well. Like Esme.

In the kitchen, Mami is packing lunches for Coco

and me while Papi is feeding Carlos his oatmeal. Somehow it is even messier than the fideo.

"Have you thought about what you might like to give Esme as a welcome gift?" Mami asks. "The tardeada is coming up soon. I'm surprised you haven't already given me a list. You're usually so organized."

I sit down next to Coco and serve myself some oatmeal. "Actually, I don't think I want to go anymore." I try to make my voice sound breezy. Like it's no big deal.

It doesn't work. Mami freezes with one hand on the open refrigerator door. Papi puts down the spoonful of oatmeal he was about to feed Carlos. Coco's mouth hangs open, even though it is full of toast.

"But you were so mad when you thought you weren't invited," Coco says.

"I wasn't *that* mad," I say, stirring my oatmeal because I don't want to look at their faces. "And anyway, I need to color-coordinate my closet on Saturday. All my clothes are out of order."

Mami frowns. "But you can do that any weekend."

Coco rolls her eyes. "She does that *every* weekend."

I stick my tongue out at her. "At least I wear fresh clothes every day. Unlike *you*."

She is still wearing that smelly old flannel.

"I told you," Coco says. "It's lucky."

Mami takes a banana from the bowl on the counter and zips up her purse. "Pues, we won't make you go to the party," she says. "But I'm disappointed that you want to miss this chance to welcome Esme to the neighborhood."

Papi nods. "Especially since you were so looking forward to meeting her."

What a mess. Not only has Jazmín turned the class against me, but now Mami and Papi are disappointed too. I want to tell them what happened, but

they'll probably just say I've been too quisquillosa.
It's a fun word to say: kee-skee-YO-sah. But it's not
so fun once you know what it means. "Persnickety."
In other words, "picky."

"I'll think about it," I promise.

Papi smiles and feeds Carlos another bite of
oatmeal.

Mami walks over and gives my shoulders a
squeeze. "Bueno," she says. "That's all I ask."

I'm not very hungry, so after two more swallows
of oatmeal, I put on my backpack. "I'm leaving for
school," I say.

"Hold up!" Coco answers. "I'll come with you as
far as the corner."

This time I wait for her.

When we get outside, Coco drops her skateboard
onto the sidewalk and hops on. She pushes slowly
alongside me until we are halfway down the block.

"So what's the real reason you don't want to go to the party?" she asks. "Is Esme weird or something? Is she *mean*?"

I can't hold it in anymore. "No!" I burst out. "But she thinks *I* am. And now everyone else does too." I explain what happened, how Pablo and I were only trying to be friendly, but everything went wrong.

We reach the corner. Coco slows her skateboard to a stop, flicks it up, and catches it under her arm. I notice a Valle Grande Elementary School sticker on the bottom of the board.

"Shouldn't you have a middle school sticker now?" I ask.

Coco rubs the sticker with her thumb. "I don't know," she says. "It makes me feel better having the elementary school sticker with me. Kind of like my flannel."

The crosswalk signal lights up. It's time for Coco

to go in one direction and me to go in the other.

"Listen," Coco says before she jumps back onto her board. "It sounds like Esme and Jazmín can't tell that you were only trying to be friendly. Maybe you can find a way to *show* them."

CHAPTER 11

Surprise Sewing

Coco's advice reminds me of what Tía Abuela told me earlier in the week. How you can see what's on someone's face, but not always what's in their heart.

Pablo thought Jazmín was being rude to us—and she kind of *was*. But it wasn't part of an evil plot. In her heart, she was trying to look out for her cousin.

Just like how Esme and Jazmín might think Pablo and I are being persnickety. But, really, we're just trying to be friends.

By the end of the school day, I think I've figured out a way to show them. I ask Pablo to meet me at the library.

"This is a pleasant surprise," Josefina the Librarian says when we get there. "But since I wasn't expecting you, I'm afraid I've already shelved most of the books."

Putting books back precisely where they belong is one of our favorite things to do at the library. Josefina usually saves them for us.

"That's okay," I say. "That's not why we're here."

"It's not?" Pablo and Josefina say together.

"I thought you were trying to cheer me up," Pablo says, shaking his head. "It was working."

"Don't worry," I tell him. "This is even better. Señora Josefina, I know we don't have a Stitch and Share meeting today, but can Pablo and I use some fabric from the scrap bin? I have an idea."

Josefina looks around the library. Ernest, her assistant, is leading a coding class. Some high schoolers are finishing their homework. In the lobby, a visitor is admiring a shimmering green gown that used to belong to Tía Abuela. She donated it to the library over the summer, and it reminds me that strong stitches aren't just for fashion. They're also for fixing. Maybe they can even fix friendships.

"It sure looks like a good time for a surprise sewing session to me!" Josefina says.

When she gets back with the bin, I reach in and pull out two pieces of flowered fabric I noticed during Stitch and Share.

"There's a new girl at school, and we want to welcome her," I explain. "She keeps drawing a picture of a house with lots of flowers in the front. I think it must be where she used to live, and I bet she misses it. If I make her a pillowcase with this flowery fabric, maybe it will remind her of home. The way the kitten pillowcase reminded you of Guapa." And the way Coco's sticker reminds her of Valle Grande Elementary.

Josefina doesn't say anything for a few long moments. I watch the second hand on her cat-shaped watch tick by. I worry that she won't let us use the fabric after all. Or that she thinks it's a terrible idea.

But then she claps her hands together. "Fantástico! It's a good thing you've sewn so many pillowcases. You're practically an expert now."

I *am*. And this pillowcase is going to be my best yet. I sit down with the fabric at one of the study tables and take the cookie-tin sewing kit out of my backpack. "Vamos! Let's get started! Sit down, Pablo. I'll teach you."

Pablo does not sit down.

"Aren't you forgetting something?" he asks. "What about Jazmín? She won't let us near her cousin."

He has a point.

"Well . . . ," I begin. "We . . . could . . . make a present for Jazmín too! Maybe that will change her mind."

As soon as I've said it aloud, I know it's a perfect plan. I hop to my feet and rummage through the scrap bin. Josefina really needs to organize all this fabric.

"A *dinosaur* pillowcase," I say.

Josefina clears her throat. "You can make as many pillowcases as you like," she says. "But I'm afraid you won't find any dinosaur fabric in there."

Pablo reaches into the bin. "No problem!" he says. "There's lots of plain fabric. I can *draw* some dinosaurs on it."

"You know," Josefina says, "I think I even have some fabric markers left over from one of our craft workshops."

While Josefina goes to look for the markers, Pablo heads into the Prehistoric Life section of the library to look for books about dinosaurs.

"I want them to be perfect," he says.

"Just make sure you draw a stegosaurus *and* a tyrannosaurus," I say. Then I smooth out my fabric and start measuring.

CHAPTER 12

Right on Time

When she finds out what I'm up to, Mami lets me stay up an hour past my bedtime to work on the pillowcases. It still takes me until Friday night to finish.

Before wrapping them up, I admire the stitches. Nice and strong. I wish Tía Abuela were here to see them. I know she'd be proud, and not just of my sewing.

On Saturday, the day of the tardeada, Pablo

meets me on the sidewalk outside Jazmín and Esme's house, exactly as we planned.

His hands are jammed into his pockets. His eyes dart nervously left and right.

"Right on time," he says when he sees me.

In other words, we are early. The party won't start for another thirty minutes.

"Of course I am," I say. Together we walk toward the house. The back gate is open, and a sign on it says BIENVENIDOS! COME RIGHT IN!

Already the sound of party music and the smell of carne asada cooking on a grill spill over the yard.

Pablo pauses. "Are you sure about this?" he asks. "What if Jazmín is mad that we came? What if she wants us to leave?"

That would be even worse than what happened at school. For a second I hesitate too. I wish I had come incognito.

But then Esme and Jazmín wouldn't be able to see what's on my face *or* in my heart.

"We don't have to stay if they don't want us to," I tell Pablo. "We'll just give them our gifts and leave. That's what we really came for, after all."

We each take a deep breath and step through the gate.

In the backyard Jazmín is spreading out a tablecloth, and Esme is hanging a papel picado banner. Jazmín stops to help Esme tie off one end, but then she notices us and lets it flutter to the ground.

"I didn't expect to see *you* here," Jazmín says.

Señora Galindo walks out the back door carrying a bowl full of tortilla chips in one arm and a vase of flowers in the other. She arranges them on one of the tables.

"Don't be silly." She turns to Pablo and me. "Of course we expected you. Maybe not this early, but you're just in time to help Jazmín and Esmeralda with the decorations. I'm going to start mixing the punch."

Señora Galindo goes back inside. Jazmín tosses a bag of balloons at me. "I guess you can blow these up while Esme and I finish hanging the banner."

Pablo and I set the gift bags down. We each pull a balloon from the plastic bag and start blowing. Esme and Jazmín take the papel picado to the other end of the patio.

"This isn't working," Pablo whispers.

I let go of my balloon. It whirs to the ground with a sad whoosh.

That's how I feel. Like all the air has sputtered out of my great idea.

It looks like I'm going to have to be bold. Like Tía Abuela. (Although, I can't help but think it would be easier with a pair of cat-eye sunglasses.)

I pick up the gift bags and walk over to Jazmín and Esme.

"We won't stay if you don't want us to," I say. "We're only here to drop off these presents. We made them ourselves." I hold out the gift bags. Jazmín and Esme exchange cautious glances before taking them.

Esme opens hers first. Carefully she removes the tissue paper and pulls out the pillowcase. She runs her fingers over the pink flowers on the front, then

flips it over to look at the red flowers on the back. I have to slap my hand over my mouth to stop myself from asking if she likes it. It feels like forever until she says anything.

"My house—the house we used to live in—had a big garden in front with pink and orange roses," Esme says finally. "This reminds me of them. How did you know?"

"I saw you drawing those flowers, and I guessed it was your old house," I say. "I didn't mean to hurt your feelings."

"I thought you were teasing me about my drawing," Esme says. "I guess I was wrong."

Now I twist some of *my* hair. "Well, we did get a little overexcited, and we probably should have given you some space since Jazmín did tell everyone you were shy," I admit. "Sorry about that."

Esme smiles.

"Aren't you going to open yours?" Pablo asks Jazmín.

She takes the pillowcase out of the gift bag and shakes it out. I'm really proud of this one. After Pablo drew the dinosaurs, I stitched on eyes and scales with some help from Josefina.

"Now I understand why you thought we were picking on your diorama," Pablo says, "but, I promise, we were only trying to be helpful. And you were right all along! A stegosaurus and tyrannosaurus *do* look pretty good together."

"Maybe," Jazmín says slowly, "I should have given you a chance to explain."

I spring up onto the tips of my toes. "Does this mean we can stay for the party?"

Esme rocks from her left foot to her right. "You can stay . . . *if*—"

"If?" Pablo and I say at the same time.

Esme giggles. "*If* you help us with this banner. It's all crooked!"

Pablo and I look at each other and grin. We are *just* the people for the job.

"Don't worry," Pablo exclaims, grabbing one end. "We'll make sure it's absolutely perfect!"

"We're going to need a ruler!" I shout, taking hold of the other end.

"And a level!" Pablo adds. "A laser one if you have it."

Esme shuffles backward and reaches for her braid again. Jazmín's hand moves to her hip.

Too much?

"Or . . . maybe," I say, "we'll just do the best we can without any special measuring tools."

Jazmín smiles. "That," she agrees, "sounds like a great plan."

And even though the banner is a little crooked when the other guests begin to arrive, it is still *perfectly* fine.

Turn the page for a
sneak peek at Catalina's
next magical adventure!

*f*LUTTER

It's after school on Monday, and the auditorium is filled with students practicing for the Valle Grande Elementary talent show. Auditions are at the end of this week.

I creep past a group of fourth graders, tap-dancing side by side next to a second grader performing a tae kwon do demonstration.

Behind them, Aaron Chu, a third grader in my class, rehearses his magic act. He swooshes his cape.

He waves his hands over a black top hat. He taps the edge of the hat with his wand. I watch, waiting to see what will happen.

When nothing does, Aaron peers into the hat and shrugs.

I shudder. I'd hate for my act to go wrong. That's why I'm sneaking through the auditorium. Somewhere in this room is the formula for a perfect performance, and I'm going to find it. I need to make sure my group has an amazing audition and gets picked for the show.

The best part is, none of the other kids notice me. Not really. When they look in my direction, all they see is a yellow-winged butterfly. That's because last summer my tía abuela—her name is Catalina Castañeda too—gave me a special sewing kit.

It might not *look* very special, just an old, worn-out velvet pouch. But the needle and thread inside have the power to sew magical disguises.

Over the weekend, I sewed butterfly wings onto one of my old sweaters. (It was missing a button anyway. I could have sewn on a new one, but it wouldn't have matched the others, and I can't stand it when things don't match). Then I added antennae to one of my hairbands. The perfect disfraz! Now anyone who sees me thinks I'm a butterfly. I am *incognito*.

Tía Abuela told me to save the magic for times when I *really* need it. Once my spool of silvery magical thread is gone, it's gone for good.

This is one of those times when I need my magic. After all, my bandmates and I will be performing a song that Tía Abuela made famous back when she was still a telenovela actress. We can't make any mistakes.

I flutter behind Esme Galindo and her cousin

Jazmín. They wear swirling blue skirts as they practice a folklórico dance.

Suddenly Jazmín stops in the middle of a step.

"What happened?" Esme asks. "Did you forget what comes next?"

They definitely need more practice.

Jazmín shakes her head. "No, but I thought I saw Catalina."

Uh-oh. Maybe my disfraz isn't working. I duck behind a cardboard tree some fifth graders are using as a prop in their skit.

"Shouldn't she be with her own group?" Esme asks.

"You know Catalina," Jazmín continues. "She probably wanted to give us some of her helpful hints."

Esme giggles, and they start dancing again.

I *might* have a reputation for being a bit of a perfectionist. *Who doesn't want to be perfect?* I almost wonder aloud. Instead I look over my shoulder to make sure the butterfly wings are still attached.

Tía Abuela warned me that the magic would only be as strong as my stitches. And these are coming loose! I need to get out of this disfraz before anyone else notices!

While the fifth graders argue over their lines, I yank off the wings and slip out of the sweater. I tuck everything under my arm, then step out from behind the carboard tree and find my group at the other side of the auditorium.

We call ourselves Banda La Chispa in honor of Tía Abuela. Her fans know her as La Chispa, "the spark," because she was always so bright and dazzling onscreen.

Ruthie Rosario sits behind her drum set. Soledad Beltrán has her guitar strapped over her shoulder. Pablo Blanco, my best friend—and biggest rival—stands next to his keyboard, tapping his foot. He scowls when he sees me. "You're late," he says.

Impossible. No one cares about punctuality as much as I do. Except for Pablo, that is. I look down at my watch and frown. Unfortunately, he's right.

"Only thirty-six seconds," I say.

"Thirty-seven," Pablo argues. "And anyway, late is late. Where were you?"

I hesitate. So far I haven't revealed the secret of the magic sewing kit to anyone.

Luckily, Ruthie interrupts before I have to answer.

"Cool hairband!" she says. "Animal accessories are my favorite!"

I feel the top of my head. I'm still wearing the butterfly antennae. "Um, thanks," I mumble, my cheeks turning warm. Pablo snorts. Normally I am perfectly put together.

Soledad hands me the tambourine we borrowed from the music room. "Now that we're all here," she says, "let's run through the song from the very beginning."

Ruthie taps out the rhythm with her drumsticks.

"Uno, dos, tres, cuatro!" Soledad counts. She begins to strum, then nods at Pablo, who presses down on the keys. I start shaking the tambourine. When we get to the chorus, I open my mouth to sing. Only, I can hardly keep up with Ruthie's beat.

Pablo's notes clash with Soledad's chords, and we all sound a little . . . off-key.

When the song ends, I cringe. Part of me wants to run back to that cardboard tree to hide again. Maybe we can still back out of the auditions. Then I remind myself of something Tía Abuela taught me when I was first learning to sew: progress takes practice. *And* patience. Sometimes a *lot* of patience.

"Don't worry," I reassure everyone. "We still have a few more days to get better."

"Are you kidding?" Soledad shouts. "That was amazing! And so much fun! We are obviously going to make the talent show."

But I'm not so sure.

CHAPTER 2

SPECIAL DELIVERY

I can't open the door at first when I get home from school. Something is blocking it. My older sister, Coco, probably dumped her enormous backpack in the entryway. *Again.* This is exactly why I asked Mami to install those special hooks on our bedroom wall. I thought that if the backpacks had a special place to hang, maybe Coco would stop leaving hers on the floor. It doesn't seem to be working.

"Co—" I start to complain as I shove the door

open. Then I look down. It isn't Coco's backpack that's blocking the way. It's a big box. Addressed to me! The postage on top says it came from Colombia.

And the handwriting tells me who sent it: Tía Abuela.

Ever since she retired from acting, Tía Abuela spends most of her time traveling the world. Wherever she goes, she finds a way to send packages home to Valle Grande. Last time, it was stickers for Coco's skateboard. And the time before that, a hand-carved rattle for Baby Carlos, our little brother. This time, it's something for me.

I push the box into the living room, where Papi and Coco are putting on a puppet show for Carlos. Maybe they should audition for the talent show too.

"It's about time you got home," Coco says.

"We almost couldn't resist opening that box," Papi agrees.

Carlos claps his hands, all sticky with the apple-sauce he's been snacking on. I wrinkle my nose and make a mental note not to let him touch whatever's inside the package.

"Well, what are you waiting for?" Coco asks, leaping up from the carpet and flinging the dinosaur puppets off her hands. "Open it!"

Of course I'm going to open it. But first I need the proper tools. Calmly I carry my backpack to the coffee table and set it down. I unzip the middle pouch and take out my school scissors.

Coco groans.

Then I carefully snip the tape along one side of the box. I am about to move on to the next piece of tape when Coco nudges me aside.

"This is going to take forever!" she complains. She kneels beside the box and rips off the rest of the tape with one sharp tug. "There. It's open."

I want to tell Coco that patience makes perfect, but I am just as excited as she is to see what Tía Abuela sent. I lift open the cardboard flaps. The gift is wrapped in tissue paper, with a note card sitting on top.

I take the note card out of the box and read aloud, "Mi amiga Josefina tells me you are making excellent progress with your sewing. Keep practicing! Sewing can be like magic. But remember what I've told you. The magic is only as strong as your stitches."

I can imagine Tía Abuela winking behind her cat-eye sunglasses when she wrote those lines. I glance up to see if Papi or Coco suspect that Tía Abuela was writing about *real* magic. They don't, so I keep reading, "I wanted you to have some new material for your next projects. This fabric is from the fashion shows in Medellín. I can't wait to see what you create with it!"

I set the note card down and reach into the box. Underneath the tissue paper are bundles of fabric. Once piece is icy blue and speckled with silver stars. The largest piece is purple and satiny smooth. There's a zebra print—one of Tía Abuela's favorite patterns—and a piece that shimmers with pink and gold sequins.

Papi takes a velvety green square and uses it to play peekaboo with Carlos. I'm so dazzled by all the fabric that I don't even mind him touching it. *Much*.

"She didn't say anything else?" Papi asks after his next *Boo!* "Nothing about where she's traveling next?"

"I don't think so," I answer. She hardly ever does. Sometimes we try to guess where her next postcard will come from, but it's always a surprise. Papi should know that.

Then Coco picks up the note card. "She did! There's more writing on the back!"

I yank the note from her hand. Coco is right. I can't believe I missed it. Most of the time, I have excellent attention to detail. It's why Tía Abuela trusted me with the magic sewing kit in the first place. I read on, "Maybe you can show me what you're working on when I come to visit. Your papi told me you'll be singing in the school talent show. I wouldn't miss it! You know the old saying: 'Quien canta sus males espanta.' 'Whoever sings frightens their worries away.'"

"Is this true?" I ask when I get to the end.

Papi tilts his head and thinks for a moment. "Well, singing *does* put me in a good mood," he says. "So I suppose it's true."

"I'm not asking if the *saying* is true!" I reply. "I mean what Tía Abuela wrote before that. Is it true she's coming to visit?"

Papi laughs. "Surprise!" he says. "I knew Tía Abuela would love to hear you sing. Especially since you'll be performing one of her songs."

Coco takes the zebra-print fabric and whips it around her neck like a cape. "I can finally show her my kick flip!" she exclaims. "And Tía Abuela promised to bring back pictures of the big skate parks in South America."

Even Carlos starts to clap again.

Not me. I sit there, staring at the note.

"What's the matter, Kitty-Cat?" Papi asks. "Aren't you excited to see Tía Abuela?"

I can tell him at least one thing that's the matter: he won't stop calling me "Kitty-Cat." As I've told my family about a zillion times, I'm getting too old for all this kitten stuff.

But that's not *really* what's bothering me. *Of course* I'm excited to see Tía Abuela. I'm especially excited to show her how far my sewing has come. When she started to teach me over the summer, I could barely thread a needle.

But this news has made me even *more* nervous about the talent show audition. What if Banda La Chispa doesn't get picked for the show, and Tía Abuela travels all this way for nothing?

Or worse, what if we *do* get to perform, and we're terrible?

"I'm excited," I tell Papi finally. "But the band has a lot of practicing to do. *And* I need to get to Stitch and Share."

READ & LEARN

with
simon kids

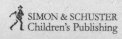

Looking for another great book?
Find it
IN THE MIDDLE.

Fun, fantastic books for kids
in the in-be**TWEEN** age.

IntheMiddleBooks.com